# THE TV KID

# THE
# TV
# KID

## Betsy Byars

Illustrated by
Richard Cuffari

The Viking Press  New York

*Copyright © 1976 by Betsy Byars. Illustrations copyright © 1976 by Viking Penguin Inc. All rights reserved. First published in 1976 by The Viking Press. A Division of Penguin Books USA Inc. 375 Hudson Street, New York, New York 10014*

*11  13  15  17  19  20  18  16  14  12*

*Library of Congress Cataloging in Publication Data. Byars, Betsy Cromer. The TV kid. Summary: To escape failure, boredom, and loneliness, a young boy plunges with all his imagination into the world of television. I. Cuffari, Richard II. Title. PZ7.B9836 Tab [Fic] 75-37944 ISBN 0-670-73331-8*

1 Lennie was in front of the motel washing off the walk with a hose. He directed the spray on a chewing-gum paper and some grass and twigs. He watched as the trash went down the drain.

A truck passed on the highway, building up speed for the hill ahead. Lennie glanced up. He watched until the truck was out of sight.

"Aren't you through yet?" Lennie's mother called. "You've got to do your homework, remember?"

He turned off the hose. "I'm through."

He started toward the office. At that moment his mom turned on the neon sign, and it flashed red above his head. THE FAIRY LAND MOTEL—VACANCY.

Lennie paused at the concrete wishing well. There was a concrete elf on one side and, facing him, Humpty Dumpty. With one hand on Humpty Dumpty's head, Lennie leaned forward and looked down into the wishing well. On the blue painted bottom lay seven pennies, one nickel, and a crumpled Mound wrapper.

Lennie walked on to the office. As he went inside, he paused in front of the TV.

A game show was on, and there were five new cars lined up on a revolving stage. The winning contestant got to pick one of the cars, and if it started, he got to keep it. Only one of the cars was wired to start.

"It's the Grand Am," Lennie said instantly. He felt he had a special instinct for picking the right box or door or car on shows like this. "I *know* it's the Grand Am."

"Lennie, are you watching television?" his mother called from the utility room.

"I'm looking for a pencil," he called back.

"Well, there are plenty of pencils on the desk."

"Where? Oh, yeah, I see one now."

Lennie was hoping to stall until he could see if it really was the Grand Am as he suspected.

The contestant said he wanted to try for the Catalina. "No, the Grand Am, the Grand Am!" Lennie murmured beneath his breath. He found the stub of a pencil on the desk and held it against his chest like a charm.

"Lennie, I meant what I said about no television," his mom called.

"I know you did."

2

"No television at all until those grades pick up."

"I know."

A commercial came on. "Doc-tor Pep-per, so mis-un-der-stoooooood."

"Me and Doctor Pepper," Lennie mumbled. He knew he had sixty more seconds to stall now. "Where did you say those pencils were?" he called.

"On the desk."

The commercial ended, and the contestant was walking across the stage to the Catalina. He was getting into the car, fastening his seat belt. At that crucial moment Lennie's mother appeared in the doorway.

"The pencils are—" She broke off as she saw him. She said sternly, "Lennie, go in my room right now and start studying."

"I will, just let me find out if it's the—"

"Now!"

In one incredibly swift move—it was like something out of an old-time movie—Lennie's mother stepped in front of him. She turned off the television. As the picture faded to one small dot, she and Lennie looked at each other.

"You didn't have to do that," Lennie said. He was hurt. He felt as if his mother had slapped him. "Now I'll never know if it was the Grand Am."

"You've got to do your homework."

"Well, will you watch for me?"

"If you go right now."

"I'm going. I'm going." He started from the office.

"Only turn the set back on or it won't warm up in time. You'll miss it."

Once outside the room Lennie stood in the hall and waited. "I wish I was on TV," he said to himself. "I wish I was getting in the Grand Am."

His mother came through the doorway. She took his shoulder and started him into her room. "It was the Firebird," she said.

"Oh." He was strangely disheartened. "Then I wish I was getting in the Firebird."

"Well, you won't be getting in anything till those grades pick up," his mom said.

"If you're thinking I'm too dumb to be on TV—well, half the people you see on those shows are dropouts. Most of the contestants are out of work."

"Len, will you please go in my room and start studying," his mom said tiredly. "I simply cannot argue with you this way every night."

"I'm going."

As he went, he thought of himself getting in the Firebird, fastening the seat belt, turning the key. He thought of his face lighting up as the engine started.

However, he thought, walking slower, if he could go on just one game show, it had better be something like *Let's Make a Deal,* where knowledge didn't count. He would dress up like a pizza, and if he got in the Big Deal of the Day, he would go for Curtain Number 2.

"Don't stall, Lennie."

"I'm not stalling." He walked into his mother's room.

His mom had set up a card table in the corner, and Lennie had to study there these days. It was the only place in the motel where there was nothing to do and nothing to look at. He couldn't even see out the window without getting up and walking around the bed.

His mother was still standing in the doorway. Lennie glanced at her. He said, "If you're thinking that I'm too ugly to be on television—well, you don't have to worry about that either. The uglier you are these days, the better. Ugliness is in."

"Start with Science."

"Mom, have you ever had a look at that kid on all those meat-spread commercials? I know I look as good as him, and they say he makes thousands of dollars."

"Lennie."

"He gets three hundred and twenty dollars for every one of those commercials. Think of it. The kid is sitting at home, probably watching himself on TV, and he's making three hundred and twenty dollars."

"Lennie—"

"And if you get on a soap opera, Mom, if you just walk in front of the camera, which anybody could do, for that you get fifty-one dollars. If you have five lines, you get ninety."

"Lennie, stop this and get to your work."

" 'Course, five dollars goes to your agent and twenty goes into a trust fund for when you get too old to perform. I read that in *TV Guide*."

"Lennie!"

"All *right!*"

They stared at each other for a moment. Then with a sigh Lennie flipped open his Science book. He turned to the chapter on plants. There was a pencil hole in the page where in anger he had stabbed the book.

With his mother watching, he stared down at the cross section of a plant. To give the illusion that he was serious about studying, he put his finger on the first part of the leaf. Slowly he moved his finger down the page, around the pencil hole.

His mom watched a moment more, and then she turned and went back into the office.

Lennie kept his eyes on the page. As he got to the picture of the stem, his eyes began to close. His mind drifted to more pleasant things. He saw his own face on TV, a close-up.

He would make the perfect contestant, he thought. In the first place, he was eager and enthusiastic. In the second place, he was a little dumb, so the audience would be glad when he won. And third, he was such a good sport he would go along with anything.

As the parts of the plant grew dimmer in his mind, his own face on TV grew sharper and clearer. The announcer's voice, hushed with urgency, replaced the sound of the trucks on the highway.

He dreamed.

2 "And now, Lennie, you have won over three thousand dollars in cash and merchandise, and, more important, you have won the chance to spin our Vacation Wheel. How do you feel about that, Lennie?"

"Real good, sir."

"Then join me over here at the Vacation Wheel. Now, Lennie, I don't have to remind you that up there on the wheel are twenty all-expense paid vacations to places all over the world, do I?"

"No, sir."

"You can go to Rome, to London, to Paris. You can go to beautiful Hawaii, exotic Mexico, or sunny Spain. All in all, there are twenty wonderful all-expense paid vacations up there on the wheel. But, Lennie, as you know, there are also what we call our zonk trips. How do you feel about those, Lennie?"

"Well, I hope I don't get one."

"And that's what we're hoping too, aren't we, folks? Hear that applause, Lennie? They're all with you. Now the three zonk trips, as we call them, are here, here, and here. Try not to land on them."

"I will, sir."

"All right, put up your hand now, Lennie, right here on the Vacation Wheel, and, Lennie, *give it a spin!*"

"Here goes!"

"Good boy! Lennie really gave it a good spin, didn't he, folks? Where do you want to go, Lennie?"

"Any of those places is all right with me."

"Except the zonk places, right?"

"Right."

"It's still spinning, and now it's beginning to slow down. Watch the wheel, folks. Where is Lennie going? To Paris? Rome? London? It's almost stopped. It looks like *Egypt!* No! *Rio!* No! *Oh, no!* Look at that! Lennie, you have landed on Number Thirteen. One of our zonk trips, and I don't have to tell you what that means."

"It means I'm going to have to take a zonk trip."

"Right."

"Where?"

"Well, let me look in my zonk envelope. Oh, Lennie."

"What?"

8

"*Oh,* Lennie."

"What? What is it?"

"*Oh, Lennie!*"

"What? I want to know. What is it?"

"Lennie, you are going to have to spend one full night —are you ready for this?—in a *haunted house!*"

"A what?"

"Yes, Lennie, you heard correctly, you are going to Haunted House Number Thirteen, located right on the outskirts—that's the dark, scary outskirts, I might add— of beautiful downtown—"

"But I don't want to spend the night in any haunted house."

"Of course you don't, but you take your chances, Lennie, just like all the other contestants. Remember that paper you signed when you came on the show?"

"Yes, but I didn't—I mean I couldn't—I mean—"

"Oh, all right, Lennie, I'll tell you what I'm going to do. You go to the haunted house, spend one night there, and if you survive—I say, *if* you survive—then you come back next week and we'll let you spin the Vacation Wheel again. How about that?"

"But, sir, couldn't I just take my three thousand in cash and merchandise and—"

"How many want to see him take the cash and merchandise and go home?"

Silence.

"How many want to see him go to the *haunted house?*"

Wild applause.

"But, sir—"

"See, the audience is with you. Hear that applause? Well, it's time for a commercial break now, but stay with us, folks, for the second half of *Give It a Spin,* the show where *you* pick your prizes and *we* see that you take them...."

3 "Lennie?"

His eyes snapped open as quickly as a puppet's. He said, "Yes'm."

"Have you finished your Science?" His mother was standing in the doorway, her hands in her jeans pockets.

"Practically."

"You know all the parts of the leaf?"

"I think so."

"And the stem?"

"I think so. I get mixed up on some of them."

"Which ones?"

"These." He made a circular motion that took in the entire page.

"Well, as soon as you're sure of them, Lennie, you bring your book in the office and let me call out the questions." She sighed. "I wish that man was still in three-fourteen— the one from Decatur, remember? Now, that was a smart man. He could have helped you with your Science."

Lennie didn't answer.

"And that man was a slow starter just like you, Lennie. He told me he didn't learn a thing until he was eleven years old. He said people thought there was something wrong with him."

Lennie didn't answer.

His mom paused. Then she said, "I don't want you getting another bad grade on your test tomorrow."

"I don't want to get one either," he said.

His last Science grade had been 23 out of a possible 100. Staring down at that 23—it had been written in red pencil and circled—Lennie had for the first time felt the real meaning of numbers. His arithmetic teachers had been trying to get that across for years—numbers *mean* something. Well, the arithmetic teachers were right, he had thought. A number, just a *number,* could ruin a person's whole day, week maybe.

Lennie had not started feeling like himself again until he was home watching a rerun of *The Lucy Show,* in which Lucy thought Mr. Mooney had turned into a monkey. When Lucy came back from lunch, saw the monkey sitting at Mr. Mooney's desk, and staggered back with her mouth open—that was when Lennie had smiled for the first time since Science.

As Lennie's mother went to the office, Lennie rested his chin on his hand and stared at the pictures. The leaf, like something in a dream, moved farther away. Slowly Lennie closed his eyes. His mind, like an unmoored ship, drifted to other shores.

The interruption by his mother was like a station break. . . . "And now," the announcer said in Lennie's mind, "back to *Give It a Spin*."

"Ladies and Gentlemen, this is Dink McLeod again. Now that our young contestant is gone, I want to let you in on a little surprise we have planned for him.

"See, our staff has concealed in that haunted house— the haunted house where Lennie will be spending the night—thirteen of the scariest, most terrifying movie and television monsters of all time. We have Dracula and Frankenstein's monster. They're in the living room. The werewolf is in the kitchen. The mummy is in the sewing room, and out in the back yard, folks, will be Godzilla, Mothro, Scorpo, and a Giant Behemoth! How about *that* for a scary quartet?"

Applause.

"We'll have hidden cameras in every room of the house to catch Lennie's reactions, so you won't want to miss our next show. Remember now, tune in next week to see what it's going to be like for young Lennie in Haunted House Number Thirteen."

"Lennie?" his mom called from the motel office.

"Yes'm?"

"I'm taking some extra towels to three-sixteen. I'll be right back."

"Yes'm."

"I'll call out the questions then."

"Right."

He didn't open his eyes. He didn't want schoolbooks and Science and his unfortunate position at the card table to intrude on his dream.

He smiled to himself. He was thinking of entering the living room of the haunted house. What a sight he would be! His knees would be trembling, his heart pounding. His eyes would be rolling around in his head like marbles. He would be holding out his hands in a blindly terrified way. He would bump into Dracula.

"Gut e-ven-ing!"

Lennie would glance up. He wouldn't have seen Dracula because of the black outfit. Now he would see the white face.

"Velcome."

Lennie's eyes, bulging almost out of their sockets, would see that Dracula's fangs were bared. His black cape was raised. Dracula would bend low, aiming for Lennie's neck.

Lennie would scream, turn, run for the door, and crash right into Frankenstein's monster. Before the huge, unmatched hands could close around Lennie's throat, Lennie would scream again and make a headlong dash for the safety of the kitchen.

He would lean against the pantry, eyes closed, catching his breath. His hands would be clutched over his pounding heart. Suddenly Lennie would feel something furry beside him. He would open his eyes. At that moment he would look out the window and see the full moon. A werewolf's moon. And the something furry beside him had to be . . . Very slowly, making no sudden moves, Lennie would ease to the door. Then, abruptly, he would rush into the sewing room and slam the door.

"I'm back, Lennie. Are you ready for me to call out the questions?"

"No, leave me alone for a few more minutes."

"But—"

"I'm almost through."

He began speeding up his dream. He thought of himself running out of the back door of the house into the yard. It would be dark despite the full moon, and in a panic Lennie would dash straight into Godzilla's big toe.

He thought of himself falling back, gasping with fright. He would stagger around Godzilla's instep, and plunge straight into Mothro's wings.

After narrowly escaping being fluttered to death, he would have a long, panic-stricken dash to Scorpo, the scorpion as big as a Boeing 747. Lennie would cringe there, too scared to move, awaiting the fatal sting.

At that moment a voice would come on the loudspeaker concealed in the trees. "Lennie, Lennie, can you hear me?"

He would be too frightened to recognize his own name. "No, no, not Scorpo!" he would be sobbing. "Anyone but Scorpo! I'm allergic to stings."

"Lennie, can you hear me? This is Dink McLeod, and

I'm here with our *Give It a Spin* audience, and, Lennie, we have had hidden cameras on you ever since you got to the Haunted House."

"You've had cameras on *me*?"

"That's right, Lennie."

"The whole time?"

"Lennie, we got the whoooooooole thing."

He would realize then what a pitiful sight he must be. Here he was cringing on the ground, sobbing at Scorpo's feet like an infant. He would raise his head. He would give a shaky laugh. He would dry his eyes on his shirt.

"Did you have hidden cameras in the house too?" he would ask.

"That's right, Lennie."

"In the—er—sewing room too?" He would remember how he had come into the sewing room and tried to hide behind the mummy, which in the dark had looked like a ragged sewing form.

"The sewing room too. We're just sorry you didn't go upstairs, Lennie, because upstairs we had the Son of Frankenstein, and the Blob, and the Creature from the Black Lagoon."

"Gee, I'm sorry I didn't get up there too."

"And now, Lennie—"

"Lennie!" It was his mom. "Bring the book out on the porch. These two schoolteachers from Wilmington checked in, and they say they'll help you."

"In a minute."

"They haven't got all night, Lennie." She sounded impatient.

"I'm on my way."

He sat with his eyes closed, speeding up his dream even more.

"And now, Lennie, we have a car waiting to bring you back to our studio to collect over three thousand dollars in cash and merchandise. How does that sound to you?"

"Real good, sir."

"And, more important, you get another spin of the Vacation Wheel."

"Oh, well, never mind about that, sir. I'll just take my cash and—"

"We'll leave it up to the audience. How many want to see Lennie come in and take his cash and merchandise?"

Silence.

"How many want to see him spin the Vacation Wheel?"

Wild applause.

"See, the audience is all with you, so come on in, Lennie, and *give it a spin!*"

"Lennie! These schoolteachers are leaving for Nashville at seven o'clock in the morning!"

"Yes'm."

Lennie rose. He picked up his book. As he carried it through the motel office to the porch, he went over the strange words for the first time . . . petiole . . . stipule. . . .

4 Lennie leaned over his desk, pencil in hand, waiting for the Science tests to be passed out. He always got a worried feeling when he was waiting to take a test. Even if he knew everything there was to know about a subject—something that had never happened—he knew he would still be worried.

He erased a mark on his desk and then penciled it back. He beat out a rhythm from *The Addams Family,* snapping his fingers when he got to the two clicks. He jiggled his leg. He turned to the boy sitting next to him and said, "Hey, Frankie, is the petiole the stem or is the stipule the stem? I'm mixed up."

Frankie shrugged.

He turned around. "Letty Bond, is—"

"The petiole is the stem," she said in a bored voice, "the stipules are extra leaves." She clicked open her ball-point pen.

Lennie turned back to the front of the room and raised his hand. "Miss Markham?"

"Yes, Lennie."

"Can we take our tests in pencil or do we have to have a ballpoint pen?"

"Pencil's fine."

"But can we use pen if we want to?" He asked this on behalf of Letty Bond, who, he thought, might be growing anxious.

"Either one is fine."

Lennie's throat was dry. The tests were coming. He put down his pencil, wiped his hands on his shirt, and picked up his pencil. He took the tests from the girl in front of him, selected the top one, and passed the rest to Letty Bond.

"Well, here we go," he said with false liveliness. He glanced at Letty Bond. She had already written her name at the top of the page and was ready to take on the first question.

Lennie turned back to his desk. The test was mimeographed in purple ink, and for a moment Lennie had a vision of another red 23 at the top of his. He let out his breath in one long unhappy sigh. He felt like writing the 23 there and saving Miss Markham the trouble.

Glancing down the page, he decided to skip the first part, which was fill-in-the-blanks, and go on to the second part, which was a plant with all the parts to be labeled. He had done that last night for the schoolteachers—two times.

Very carefully he printed the word "petiole" in the line opposite the stem. Then he looked at the word. It looked wrong. Quickly he turned his pencil and erased the word. He wet his lips. He wanted to turn around and ask Letty Bond if she was sure the petiole was the stem. It seemed to him . . . Nervously he printed "petiole" back in the same space.

He printed in four more words, and then he got up. With his eyes on his paper, he went to the teacher's desk. "Miss Markham?"

"Yes, Lennie."

"Is that word spelled right?"

"I'm sorry, but I can't give you any help after the tests are passed out."

"Oh." He stood there for a moment staring down at the word he had written. "Stupile." He had never felt more miserable in his life. He gave Miss Markham a weak smile. He said, "I feel kind of stupile myself today."

"I do believe, though," Miss Markham went on kindly, smiling back at him, "you should look at what you've written *very* carefully. There may be something wrong."

"Thank you, Miss Markham."

As Lennie hurried back to his desk, Miss Markham said, "Remember, spelling counts, class."

Lennie erased the word and respelled it. He filled in two more blanks and erased one. His test now had a worked-over look. He had worn through the paper in two places. He thought that anyone who thinks school isn't hard ought to take a look at this paper.

He bent over his desk, wet his pencil point, and filled in another blank. He went on to the multiple-choice section and filled in three of those. He glanced again at the word "stepile."

"Time's up, class," Miss Markham said.

Lennie looked up, startled. He turned to Frankie. "Are you through?"

Frankie shrugged.

"Are you through, Letty Bond?"

"I've been through since ten thirty," she said. He glanced at her desk. She was writing a note to someone named Anne. It started out: "Am I bored!"

Lennie spun around and glanced in desperation at his test. Only half of the blanks were filled. Quickly he began filling in the rest, guessing, putting anything down so that Miss Markham would see a full, completed sheet when she got to his test. That was bound to make a better impression.

"Lennie." It was Miss Markham.

"Yes'm." He kept writing. He did not have time to look up.

"I have to have your test now."

"Yes'm."

"The next class is coming in."

"One more word." In desperation Lennie kept writing. Cammie Hagerdorn was standing by his desk, waiting to take Lennie's seat. Lennie looked up.

"Hard, huh?" Cammie said.

"Hard for me." Lennie sighed. He got up, dropped his test on Miss Markham's desk, and went out into the hall. Shoulders sagging, he went slowly to World Studies.

5 "How'd you do on your Science test?" His mom didn't glance up as he came in the office door. She was looking at the guest register. She was going over the names carefully, as if she were hoping they would multiply like amoebas and fill the page.

"Oh, all right."

"Really?" She looked up, smiling.

"I think so."

"I *knew* you'd do well." She leaned forward on her arms. "And it wasn't the schoolteachers either—it was all that studying you did."

He glanced at the TV set. Farmer Fred was on. He was

yelling, "Pull up your milking stools, boys and girls, and get set for Farmer Fred and his cartooooons!"

Slowly Lennie started back to his room. The sounds of the first cartoon washed over him. It was Tweetie Bird and Sylvester. Tweetie Bird was crying, "I *did!* I taw a *putty tat!*"

His mom called, "Oh, Lennie, would you take a roll-away bed to three-fourteen?"

"Yes'm."

As he came back through the office, pushing the bed, he saw that Sylvester was sawing a hole in the ceiling over Tweetie Bird's cage. Lennie walked more slowly.

"The bed, Lennie."

"Just let me see him fall to the floor."

Sylvester finished his circle in the ceiling and fell with a crash to the floor. He pulled himself up in the shape of a round paper doll.

"I'm *going,*" he said before his mother could remind him again.

He pushed the bed out the door. There were three rooms occupied at the motel that afternoon. A farmer with a station wagon of roosters was in 310. A salesman was in 316. A family of five had just checked into 314.

Lennie knocked at the door. "Here's the bed," he called out.

"Come in."

Lennie opened the door and pushed the bed into the room. The television was on, and Lennie glanced quickly at it to see if he could catch the ending of the Sylvester cartoon.

26

On the screen a man in a chef's suit was teaching the number three by juggling three pizzas. "*Three,*" he said.

A girl of about five was sitting on the edge of the bed, watching the chef. Her mouth was open a little.

"Cartoons are on Channel Seven," Lennie said as he unfolded the bed.

The chef took another pizza and started juggling. "*Four,*" he said.

"Will that be all?" Lennie asked formally.

The woman nodded, and Lennie turned to the door. The chef cried, "*Five!*" and the woman said, "See what else is on."

Lennie turned. He said, "We get *Farmer Fred's Cartoons, Gilligan's Island, Bonanza,* and Mike Douglas."

"Oh. Thank you."

"Sure."

Lennie started back to the office. His mother was sitting in one of the webbed chairs on the porch. It was her favorite time of the day—when she could sit out and chat with the guests. Now she was talking to the salesman in 316.

"I delivered the bed," Lennie said.

She turned to him, her face bright. "Lennie, guess what this man sells?"

"I don't know."

"Encyclopedias!"

"Oh."

"Why, you should have been here last night." She turned back to the salesman. "We had a regular school going out here, didn't we, Lennie?"

"Yes."

She looked at him. She said, "Listen, you go on in and watch TV if you like."

"I thought I wasn't allowed."

"You deserve it for doing so well on your Science test."

"Oh, all right."

Lennie went into the office and sank down on the plastic sofa. He reached for the TV knob. He began to feel a little better. He said to himself, I think I'll see what Hoss and Little Joe are up to. He leaned back on the plastic. It felt good and cool. He put his feet up on the plastic coffee table. He sighed with contentment.

6 Lennie came out the back door of the motel. Here lay the broken Fairy Land figures—the dwarfs and fairies that had been out in front of the motel until they crumbled. Lennie stepped around an armless Red Riding Hood and a headless fairy godmother.

He climbed down the hill behind the motel and crossed the field. It was a Saturday, a bright October morning, and he had finished his chores at the motel. Usually he sat in the office on Saturday mornings and watched cartoons, but this morning he felt the need to get away.

The day before he had gotten his Science test back, and he had made a 59. The thought of that 59 still made him feel sick. Only 11 more points and he would have passed like everyone else.

As soon as he had seen that 59, he had thought there should be some kind of patent medicine for moments like this. This had to be worse than acid stomach and sinus headache and low backache all rolled into one.

"For that uncomfortable feeling that comes when you fail your Science test, take Fail-Ease, the tablet that eases failure and makes you less afraid to fail the next time."

He would be on the commercial, sitting right at his desk in Science class, pale and sick. He would drop two Fail-Ease tablets into a glass of water, drink, and a wonderful feeling of relief would come over him. The lines of tension in his face would relax. Color would come back to his cheeks.

The teacher would walk back to his desk. She would lean down, smiling, and say, "I hope you've learned, Lennie, that with Fail-Ease you never have to feel the pain of failure again."

"Yes," he would say, "for relief from the nagging pain of failure—" and then he and Miss Markham would smile at each other and say together, "take Fail-Ease, the failure reliever that requires no prescription."

The thought had raised Lennie's spirits for a moment. Then Miss Markham had rapped on her desk and said, "I want these tests signed by one of your parents, students, and returned on Monday."

Lennie had brought his test home and stuck it in his sock drawer. His mom had been too busy to ask about it

—they had had seven rooms occupied at the motel that night—but sooner or later she would. And even if she didn't, Lennie would have to get her to sign it.

It was something he couldn't bear to do. When he disappointed his mother with his school work, her mouth got as sad as a clown's.

"This is our big chance, Lennie," she had been saying ever since she had inherited the Fairy Land Motel from her father. They had been heading for the motel on a Trailways bus the first time she had said it. "This is our big chance, Lennie. All a person can hope to get in this life is one good chance."

He had nodded, smiling at her. He had been as pleased about inheriting the motel as she was.

"Now we can live like other people," she had said. She had begun to hum. Her favorite songs were about home and going home. Now she was humming "Country Roads." She stopped humming long enough to say, "You'll go to school regularly and make good grades— no more of this moving around."

They looked like people who moved around, Lennie thought, both in jeans and T-shirts, his mother's hair frizzled and his own uncut. But no more.

"And I'll make a success of the motel. I promise you that."

"And I'll be a success in school," he'd said.

As he sat there on the bus, he saw himself as the end of a TV show. All his problems and troubles were over. The last crisis had been passed. He and his mom were heading for home and happiness. It was as perfect as the ending of a Lassie show. He saw himself smiling while the credits rolled past his beaming face.

Only that was the trouble with life, Lennie had found out later. He had expected things to change as quickly and dramatically as they did in bad-breath commercials—one gargle and a new life. It hadn't worked that way.

In real life, Lennie found out, problems didn't get wrapped up neatly between commercials. In real life you moved, and all the things that were wrong with you moved with you. If you couldn't pass Science in Kentucky, then you wouldn't be able to pass it in Tennessee either.

Lennie wondered if this happened to other people, like Presidents of the United States or famous TV stars. Did they get their lifelong ambition, thinking life would be perfect when they got to be President or when they got their own series, and then find out that all the things wrong with them were still wrong?

Lennie walked quickly down the hill. He had come this way so often that there was a faint path in the deep grass. He came to the maple trees—the leaves were solid gold now, and he walked up the next hill. At the top were the ruins of two old campfires, black circles like a puff of breath from a dragon.

The first time Lennie had seen the old fires, he had paused and planned a TV show about a dragon. Only one person, himself, knew about the dragon. He had trailed the dragon to his cave by following these double campfires, and the dragon and he had become friends.

The highlight of the program came when the townspeople arrived at the cave to kill the dragon, thinking him responsible for the recent slaughter of sheep.

"Get out of the way, son. We're going in."

"But the dragon's my friend. He wouldn't kill anything!"

"There's seventeen sheep dead in the valley. Somebody killed them."

"Well, *he* didn't do it. He couldn't."

"Get out of the way, son. We got no quarrel with you."

"But he *couldn't* have killed the sheep, I tell you! He doesn't have any *teeth!*"

"What?"

"He's over two hundred years old, and all he eats is bananas and tomatoes and once in a while a real ripe apple."

"Listen! The boy might be telling the truth! Seems to me my gran'daddy said there was a dragon around here when he was a boy."

"Your gran'daddy Amos?"

"My gran'daddy Amos, and I recall him saying that dragon never hurt a fly."

"Well, then, maybe it was *wolves* that got them sheep. If, as the boy and your gran'daddy says, the dragon's harmless, we'll let him be."

That had been one of Lennie's favorite dreams. It had rerun for days. But now he stepped between the old fires without noticing and went down the hill beneath the red beech trees. Here the grass was as soft and green as official grass. Then he came to the lake.

He stood for a moment looking at the water, at the

places where the reflection of trees turned the water red and gold. He looked at the houses. Each of them was closed for the winter. The lake was really his now.

Lennie went into the weeds and, pulling hard, brought out his boat. He eased it into the water.

The boat was old and heavy. Someone had abandoned it long ago because the seats were half rotten and the boards leaked. When Lennie had first seen the boat, weeds were growing inside. Purple flowers were poking up over the sides as if they were waiting for a ride.

Lennie got into the boat. Old and rotten as it was, it was still sturdy enough to get Lennie across the lake. The first time he had pushed off in the boat, he had half expected to sink. He had imagined himself going down the way Coyote and Bugs Bunny and Sylvester did in old cartoons, just standing there, sinking, with a comical expression.

That was one thing he particularly liked about cartoon characters. When they walked out on a limb and the limb cracked, or they ran out on the air and then realized nothing was under them, they looked into the camera in such a comical way. If he had a camera on him, he could do the same thing.

For a moment he wished he were back at the motel watching the Saturday morning cartoons. Then, leaning on his oar, he pushed into deeper water. He began to row.

Lennie was not supposed to be here, because this was a private lake. It had been dammed up and filled for the benefit of the people who had houses here. No one else was allowed. But as long as nobody saw him—and there was nobody to see him now, he thought—it was all right. He kept rowing.

Lennie knew more about this lake and these houses than anybody else. There was not a house here that he had not entered at one time or another. Sometimes he went in through a window, sometimes through a door if he knew where the key was hidden. But however he got in, Lennie never took anything or did any damage. He just liked to look at other people's things.

There was something about strange people's houses that fascinated Lennie. Perhaps that was because he had never lived in a real house himself, only in apartments and trailers and motels.

Lennie's favorite house was the stone one with the willow trees in front. His finest hours had been spent in the tiny back room of the stone house, sitting on the floor, warmed by the sun coming in the window, playing with twenty-five-year-old Tinker Toys or dealing out games of Circus Old Maid or Animal Rummy or looking through shoe boxes of stringless Yo-Yos and stones as smooth as bird's eggs.

In the center of the lake he suddenly wished he were back at the motel again. He tried to lose himself in his thoughts.

What if the Partridge family's bus had broken down and they were stranded, and while he was rowing across the lake he started singing and they heard him and asked him to join the group and gave him his own electric

guitar. While he was imagining himself in a white fringed suit on the stage with the Partridges, he lost interest.

He shifted thoughts.

What if he were the last person on earth. He had seen that the week before on *Thursday Night Movie*. A plague had come and disintegrated everyone but one person. Now Lennie imagined himself that person, rowing across the lake, wondering what had happened to everyone else.

He rowed more slowly. His oars dragged in the water. He felt as lonely as if he really were the last person on earth.

To change his mood, he imagined a commercial. "To help that lonely feeling," the announcer would say, "buy Friend, the doll that's as big and as real as you are."

He brightened. He imagined the announcer's voice saying, "Yes, with Friend, you'll always have someone to talk to." There would be a shot of him and Friend talking and laughing on a park bench.

"With Friend, you'll never have to go to the movies alone." There would be a shot of him and Friend entering a theater. The announcer would say quietly, "And remember, Friend comes with a special ID card that lets him enter all movie theaters and sports events for half price."

Lennie smiled. He began to row again. He felt better. He imagined the end of the commercial with him and Friend strolling along a country road. The announcer would say, "Yes, take Friend everywhere you go and—" Then a choir of a hundred voices would sing, "*You'll ne-ver be a-lone.*"

Lennie was close to the shore now, and he eased up on his rowing. He drifted the rest of the way. When his boat touched shore, Lennie got out quickly. He pulled his boat up under the long waving branches of the willow tree. He started for the house.

7 Lennie was on the front porch of the stone house now. He peered in the window.

In his mind the announcer reminded him, "Whenever you enter an empty house, take Friend along. Yes, remember, no house is ever empty with Friend."

He imagined Friend peering in the window too, glancing at Lennie, waiting.

"Let's go in," Lennie would say. Friend would nod in agreement. "Follow me." Another nod and Friend would fall in behind.

"Remember," the announcer would say, "with Friend there's never an argument. He does what *you* want, goes where *you* go."

The key to the front door was on top of the door molding, and Lennie took down the key and put it in the lock. He liked to enter with the key because it gave him a feeling of belonging. Going in the window wasn't as good.

He was lifting up on the doorknob when he heard a car on the road. He was startled. He thought everyone at the lake had gone back to their regular houses. He stood deerlike for a moment, one hand on the key ready to turn, one hand on the knob ready to lift.

Then his tension eased. It's just somebody who made a wrong turn, he told himself. He took a step backward and caught sight of the car. It was a blue sedan, four houses away. Lennie could just see a glimpse of it shining through the trees, but he could see that the car was moving slowly up the road, pausing at each driveway.

Lennie glanced over his shoulder at the lake. He saw the willow trees. He saw the bow of his boat poking through the leaves. Then he glanced back at the car. It was at the A-frame now, three houses away.

Silently Lennie closed the screen door, leaving the key in the lock. Bending low, he crawled to the steps. Here he hesitated again. He didn't think he could make it to his boat. And if he did, he knew he couldn't row across the lake without being spotted.

In a crouch, he went around the porch. The car was two houses away now. It was behind the house with the artificial brick siding. And for the first time Lennie got a good look at the car. It was a police car.

His fear flared. He dodged quickly around the side of

the house. He stood there a moment, flattened against the stones.

Lennie had never heard that the police patrolled this area. Maybe they didn't as a usual thing, he thought. Maybe people had complained that their houses had been bothered. Maybe they had asked the police to keep an eye out. Maybe he was going to be arrested.

The car was next door now, pausing at the driveway. Lennie was afraid he had waited too long. He glanced around, panic-stricken.

Then in one fast move he fell to his stomach and wriggled into the crawl space under the house. It was damp and musty here, a maze of discarded items and old tools and unused building materials. Cold air moved under the house, and Lennie thought he heard something scamper.

Pulling himself along with his elbows, he scooted around a pile of shutters, a box of Mason jars, and a watering can with the bottom rusted out. He was cold, and his jacket was back at the Fairy Land Motel, hanging on a hook in the office.

Lennie struck his head on a low water pipe and ducked. He was rubbing his head when he caught sight of the police car through the gap between some old plastic milk bottles and a tipped-over barrel. The police car slowed down and came to a stop at the driveway.

To calm himself, Lennie thought of Friend. It really wasn't a bad idea, a product like Friend. Girls would always have someone to dance with at parties. Old people would never be caught talking to themselves. Right now he would feel a lot better with Friend sitting beside him.

"Whenever you feel afraid, reach for Friend. His hand is always there in a plastic so lifelike you can hardly tell it from the real thing."

Lennie would touch the plastic hand, not for comfort, but to get Friend's attention. "*You* go out," he would whisper to Friend, "let them catch *you*."

One nod and Friend would crawl out, willingly surrendering, his arms outstretched for the handcuffs.

Against his will Lennie's mind turned from Friend. He could see the policeman now. He was standing by the car. He leaned down and spoke to the other policeman, who was working the radio. Lennie couldn't hear what they were saying.

He inched forward so he could see the policeman a little better. He was a big man. He had probably been strong once, but he had started going downhill. Everything about him sagged—his arms, his stomach, his neck. The other cop—Lennie could see him now too—looked like Tiny Tim with a haircut.

It was so much like a television show that for a moment Lennie half expected to see the two cops framed in an eleven-inch black-and-white set. He wished suddenly it *was* a television program and that a commercial was about to come on. All Lennie would need would be sixty seconds to get away.

The two policemen spoke again. The big cop looked up at the sky.

Lennie waited. He crossed his fingers for luck.

The policeman looked down at his shoe. Lennie thought for a moment he was getting ready to step back into the patrol car. Lennie's breath began to ease out in a long sigh of relief.

Then, abruptly, the policeman turned and headed straight for Lennie.

**8** Lennie inched closer to the large pile of stones by the chimney. He crouched behind it. He couldn't see the policeman now.

The stones he was leaning against were as round and smooth as cannon balls. These stones were what had first impressed Lennie about the house. He had felt that only very particular people would choose stones like these. Ordinary people would just settle for rough stones blasted out of a quarry. These stones—if Lennie knew anything about stones—had been hand-picked out of some creek where they had been worn smooth by about a thousand years of rippling water.

Lennie still couldn't see the policeman, but he could hear his footsteps coming closer. The policeman tried the back door, paused, took two steps to the right. He was probably looking in the kitchen window now, Lennie thought, and then the policeman came down the steps and went around the right side of the house. Lennie pressed closer to the pile of stones and put his hand on one of them for comfort.

Slowly, as if he were pacing off a distance, the policeman walked to the front of the house. Lennie could see his legs now, the crease in his pants. His shoes were as shiny as Christmas tree ornaments. If Lennie crawled closer, he could see his face in them.

The policeman stopped, and for one terrible moment Lennie expected the policeman to drop down on all fours and peer past the trash to where Lennie crouched. Lennie's face would shine in the darkness like a light bulb. "I see you, son, come on out."

But the policeman moved on to the steps. He stood there a moment, shielded by the ferns. Then, one by one, he took the stairs. He went up as slowly as a trained bear.

Lennie was almost under the porch, so he could hear every move the policeman made. The policeman looked in the living-room window, peering in for a long time like a beggar. He took in the deerhead over the mantel, the faded sofa, the big oilcloth-covered table, the electric motor somebody had left on the daybed. Lennie knew that room by heart. And if the policeman wanted to, if he bent to the left, he could see into the back bedroom, Lennie's room. He could see the chest where all Lennie's favorite things were stored.

The policeman moved to the front door. He opened the screen.

There was a silence, and Lennie knew the policeman was looking at the key in the lock, wondering what it was doing there.

"Hey, Bert," he called, "look here a minute."

The second policeman got out of the car. He walked around the house and took the steps to the porch two at a time.

"Looks like somebody was going in."

"Yeah, or trying to."

"People ought not leave their keys just lying around, careless like."

"Yeah, there ought to be a law."

Lennie rubbed his hand over the smoothest of the stones. It was so smooth it could be an old dinosaur egg, Lennie thought. Here, under his hand, fossilized for a million years, could be an embryo dinosaur that had never even had a chance at life. The idea appealed to Lennie. In good faith some dinosaur had laid this egg, expecting a tiny bright green miniature of herself to pop out, and instead it had wound up as an imitation rock under somebody's house.

It would make a nice television show, Lennie thought. The show would open with a shot of the rock under the house, and then very slowly the rock would begin to crack open and out would come the little dinosaur.

It could be as nice a farm series as *Lassie*, Lennie planned. Carol Burnett would be the farmer's wife; Tim Conway, the farmer. They would be sitting at the kitchen table when the egg hatched. Carol Burnett would feel a tremor. Her chair would bobble. She'd say, "Did you feel something?"

Tim Conway would not look up from his supper of noodles. "I didn't feel nothing," he'd say.

They'd go back to eating. The dinosaur below would have a growth spurt. His head would hit the floor. Carol Burnett's chair would fall back three feet.

"Didn't you feel something then?" she'd ask, struggling up.

"I didn't feel nothing," Tim Conway would say.

The dinosaur's head would crack the floor, sending Carol Burnett into the stove. She would pull herself out. Her wig would be sideways, her bathrobe scorched. "Did you feel something *then?*"

"I didn't feel nothing."

Suddenly the dinosaur, full-grown, would explode through the kitchen floor. Tim Conway would be sent flying through space. He would go over the barn, through the chicken coop, past the silo, and into the wood pile. He would look up, dazed. "I think I felt something," he'd say.

Afterward, Lennie thought, when the series got popular, the dinosaur could do Lassie-type things like saving babies and rescuing forest rangers.

Above him the policeman said, "Could be somebody

inside." Lennie forgot the TV show. The policeman's foot moved and a little dust shifted down through the cracks in the boards.

"We better take a look."

The policeman turned the key in the lock and pushed on the door. He didn't know that you had to lift up on the knob, Lennie thought. Then, abruptly, the door opened and the two policemen entered the house.

Lennie couldn't hear them as clearly now, but every now and then a board would creak, and Lennie would know they were in the kitchen, looking behind the hot-water heater. Or they were in Lennie's bedroom or climbing the stairs to the second floor.

"Looks like everything's in order," Lennie heard the policeman say as he came out on the porch.

"Mr. Wilkins was right, I guess, about somebody going in these houses."

"Yeah."

"Probably some kids."

"Nothing's been taken, though. It doesn't look like it, anyway."

"Not much to take, if you ask me."

In the crawl space Lennie lifted his head in surprise and almost hit the water pipe again. How little those policemen understood! Why, the objects in this house were as valuable as the contents of a museum—to him, anyway. He would give anything to have the contents of the drawers in the chest. To Lennie they would be like a mummy's possessions, special chosen things to be saved for a later life. Lennie would settle happily for just the old marbles and the Parcheesi set and the worn dominos.

The policemen came down the front steps. "If it was me, I'd rather have a place over on Paradise Lake," one said. They walked around the left side of the house. They were as perfectly in step as drilling soldiers. "That's a real nice place. You can't build a house at Paradise Lake that don't have metal siding."

They paused at the corner of the house. Lennie could see their legs perfectly now.

One of them said, "Look at that. The drain pipe's busted. The steps'll be rotten by summer."

Then they walked, still in step, to the patrol car. They got in and the little cop started the engine. Slowly, as Lennie reclined against the smooth stones, the car pulled away from the drive and moved on down the road.

9 For a moment Lennie could not move. He was weak with relief. He had been spared, saved, let off the hook. A fish probably felt like this, Lennie thought, when he was caught by Marlin Perkins for *Wild Kingdom* and then was mercifully thrown back into the water because he was too little.

"Although some fish are too little, *you* are never too little to be insured by Mutual of Omaha," Marlin Perkins would say later with a quiet smile.

Lennie thought of the rejected fish hitting the sparkling water, sinking, dropping down where the water was dark and cold, and lying there, taking himself for

51

dead. Then Lennie thought of the fish realizing that life was still there and in a burst of power going straight up, breaking the surface of the water like one of those trick porpoises at Sea World.

Lennie rested a moment more because his legs felt weak. Fright took a lot out of a person, turned the legs to rope and the heart to a caged bird.

And also Lennie was waiting. The police car had moved on around the lake, but this could be a trick. At any moment the car could make a U-turn and come back. If the policemen were suspicious, that's exactly what they would do. Lennie decided he would stay where he was for at least another fifteen minutes.

He rested against the stones. To pass the time he began to think of himself as part of TV shows. He could see the listings in *TV Guide*.

**7** **THE ROOKIES**
The cops are called to investigate a breaking and entering at a lake house. Making his TV debut is Lennie in the role of the criminal.

**2** **MEDICAL CENTER**
A young boy faces permanent injury when he is tear-gassed by the police in an attempt to get him out from under a lake house. Making his TV debut is Lennie in the role of the tear-gassed boy.

He smiled to himself. Now that his fear had lessened, now that he was sure everything was all right, the danger from the cops didn't seem real. Actually his only real worry had been about his mom. If they'd caught him . . .

If they'd driven him to the Fairy Land Motel . . . If they'd taken him into the office and said, "Ma'am, we just placed your son under arrest" . . . That *would* have been terrible.

He remembered that, only the evening before, his mom had said she was proud of him. A family of four had driven into the motel at dusk and Lennie had taken two cots to their room. He had taken ice to the couple in 316, extra linen to 304, and he had made up 311 and 313 without being told. It was, he admitted, mostly to make up for the bad grade he had gotten on his Science test, but his mom hadn't known that.

"I'm really proud of you," she had said. "All that studying the other night on Science—it will pay off too, I know it will—and all the help you're giving me tonight. We're going to make it, Lennie, I know we are."

For a moment Lennie lay there staring up at the cobwebs that had formed between the boards of the house. He was thinking about his mother.

Then out of the corner of his eyes he caught sight of movement. He straightened.

The police car was coming back. So silently Lennie hadn't heard it, moving in that slow, first-gear way, the car came to the driveway of the stone house and turned in.

**10** Lennie waited. When he did not hear the car door open, he slipped forward until he had a better view. The policemen were not getting out of the car. Perhaps they were sitting there having a smoke, Lennie thought. Maybe a late lunch. The big sagging cop was probably downing a couple of Twinkies. Lennie smiled. He imagined the cop taking a bite, looking at the other cop, saying, "Freshness never tasted so good."

The smile faded. What were the cops *doing?* Anyway, Lennie thought, it was lucky that he had stayed under the house, that he hadn't scrambled out right away. If he had, he would have been yanked up by the heels like a newborn baby. "Got you! All right, kid, tell us who your parents are."

Lennie was lying on his side now. A cobweb beneath the flooring touched Lennie's cheek, but Lennie didn't even raise his hand to brush it away. He kept his eyes on the blue strip of the car. There was still no sound or movement.

"Come on, come on, *leave!*" Lennie begged beneath his breath. He crossed his fingers, then uncrossed them. "*Leave!*"

Then, abruptly, Lennie heard the engine start. He couldn't believe it for a moment. The wheels spun a little in the dust of the drive and then the car backed up. It was moving fast.

The car backed onto the road, moved forward, and drove out of Lennie's vision. It took the first curve in the road so rapidly that Lennie could hear the squeal of tires. He smelled dust. He did not move. He waited.

Five minutes later the car got to the highway and Lennie heard the high wail of the siren as the car headed for Bennetsville.

Now Lennie relaxed for the first time since he had seen the car. It really is over now, he thought. An emergency somewhere—an accident perhaps, a criminal on the loose —and the police were called to duty.

He could crawl out in peace now. He turned onto his stomach and got set to scramble out. His left leg touched the pile of stones, and Lennie pushed himself forward.

The pushing started a small slide. The rocks shifted. A few tumbled to the ground and rolled away like balls. Mixed with the sound of the shifting, rolling stones was another sound. A rattle.

No sooner had Lennie heard it than he felt the sharp stab of fangs on his ankle.

He jerked his head around, and in the shadow of the crawl space he saw a snake. It was so nearly the color of the ground that it seemed for a moment to be the ground itself set in motion.

Instantly Lennie twisted away. He rolled over twice. When he stopped and glanced back, the snake was moving behind the tipped-over oil drum. It disappeared in the shadows.

Lennie drew his leg up to his chest and yanked up his pants. There was a yellow stain on his sock. Slowly, as carefully as if he were unwrapping something, Lennie pulled down the sock and looked at the two tiny holes in the inside of his ankle.

Drops of blood oozed out, and instinctively Lennie bent down and sucked the wound and spit out blood and venom. He did this a second time, a third, and then he drew back again and looked at the wound.

A cold chill went up his spine. He said to himself: The main thing I am not supposed to do is panic. He remembered that from when Little Joe got snake-bitten on the Ponderosa. But he knew he already had panicked. Just the sight of those two holes in his ankle had caused his heart to pound like a hammer. Blood rushed through his body with the force of Niagara Falls. His throat had tightened up. Suddenly he couldn't see because tears were in his eyes.

It seemed to Lennie then that this was the secret of life

—the thing man had always been afraid of. Even when man thought he was afraid of the Russians or the atom bomb or some new virus, what he really feared was that he would wind up bitten by a snake—two holes in his ankle. Lennie tried to see the wound through his tears.

It was man's first fear, Lennie seemed to remember, way back in the Bible, and the Bible knew how to scare a person. Lennie almost felt that this was the same snake. It had slithered down the tree in the Garden of Eden, tempted Adam, wound through deserts, around pyramids, stowed away on a banana boat, come to the United States, crossed ditches and parks and burning asphalt roads, and come here to wait for Lennie beneath the stone house.

Lennie blinked, and the two holes came into focus again. "I got to get out of here," Lennie said.

Then, using the same side-to-side motions the snake had used going behind the oil drum, Lennie pulled himself out of the shadow of the crawl space. He slid into the sunlight. He sat up.

And there in the dappled sunlight, beneath trees that were solid gold, Lennie rolled up his pants leg and took off his shoe. He stripped off the stained sock. He looked again at the two small holes in the pale flesh of his ankle.

**11** Lennie's ankle was bleeding freely now. The blood was streaming down his foot, dropping onto the dry, dusty earth. The pain had increased.

Lennie hunched over his foot. This sharp, stinging pain made him even more afraid. His heart started beating harder. His mouth got drier. He kept saying over and over, "I got to keep calm. I got to keep calm." But this seemed only to make him more frightened.

He reached into his back pocket for his knife. It was there tangled in some string and a red bandana. When he got it loose, he tried to open it one-handed as he always did, but his fingers were trembling too much.

Fumbling, using both hands, he got the knife open. Then it dropped in the dust. In a panic Lennie wiped the dusty knife blade off on his pants. He knew what to do, but he hesitated a moment. He felt physically sick now. Then he bent quickly and cut little x's over the fang marks.

He moaned. For the first time in his life he wanted to be in a hospital among people who knew what they were doing. Doctors and nurses had always frightened Lennie before, but now in his mind they took on the beauty of painted pictures.

He took three deep breaths. Then he bent down and began to draw out the blood. He spit it into the dust.

Suddenly he thought of a tourniquet, and he wrapped the bandana around his leg and tied it tight. He sucked hard at the snake bite, drawing a mouthful of blood. He spit it out.

His ankle really hurt now. It was a burning pain, sharp and stinging, as if his leg were being slashed by razor blades. He had to get help.

The telephone! Lennie thought. He got up and, hobbling on one foot, made his way around the house and up the steps. The key was gone, but Lennie went straight to the window by the sofa and pulled it up. Lucky he had known about that latch being broken.

Carefully he swung his leg over the sill. The telephone was on the far wall, and Lennie kept his eyes on it as he struggled across the room. Rainbow-like, it seemed to get farther and farther away.

Lennie held on to one piece of furniture after another —the overstuffed chair, the end table, the floor lamp. He had once thought this furniture must have come from at least twenty different people.

"Well, I can get along without this chair, I reckon," someone had said.

"I got no more use for this table."

"I was going to give this rug to the Sunday school, but if you can use it . . ."

Lennie had liked that. At the time he had thought that if he ever had a house, that's the way he would have wanted to furnish it—one piece of furniture from everybody he liked.

With a swimming motion, weaving through the furniture, he got to the phone at last. He lifted the receiver. Silence. He jiggled the piece up and down. Silence. He dialed 0. Silence. As he stood there on one foot, he seemed to get smaller in size. The phone had been disconnected for the winter.

Slowly Lennie let himself down into the first chair he came to. It was the brown overstuffed armchair, and he sank as slowly as an old rheumatic man. He didn't think he would ever get up again. He lifted his leg as gently as he could and rested it on the green plastic footstool. His ankle was turning purple.

He had so wanted to hear the voice of the operator saying, "Number, please." He had so wanted to reply, "Get me the Fairy Land Motel."

He laid his head back against the chair. There was a

picture hanging on the opposite wall. Lennie had never noticed it before. He would not have noticed it now except that the sunlight from the window was falling on it, lighting it up as if it were in a museum.

The picture was a barnyard scene painted by someone who had never been in a barnyard. No pigs were that pink. No rooster was that red. No cow went around with four golden straws in the side of her mouth.

Tears came to Lennie's eyes. They spilled over onto his cheeks and rolled down his face. He caught the first one with his tongue. He tasted the salt. Then he gave up and let the tears flow.

It would take a miracle to save him now, he thought. He couldn't walk. Any movement at all was terribly painful. The police wouldn't come back. No one knew where he was. He needed a real miracle, a twitch from Samantha's nose or a visit from the Flying Nun or a nod from Jeannie.

He had always loved those shows. When things went wrong—when Darren got changed into an elephant, Samantha would just twitch her nose and make him a man again. When Jeannie's master was accidentally sent into space instead of a rhesus monkey, Jeannie would nod him back again. That kind of magic was what he needed.

Slowly he reached down, loosened the tourniquet, let the blood flow back into his leg for a moment. Then he tightened it again.

Suddenly he thought of his mother. He knew how sad she would look when she found out. All the trouble he had caused her—all the vaccinations and school lessons and tooth fillings. She had even signed him up for safety lessons one summer at a municipal pool. She had taken him with her through seven states—and all for what? To have him sink down into an overstuffed chair and die.

Wincing with pain, Lennie got to his feet. Outside, the sun went behind a cloud, and it got dark in the room. For a moment Lennie was terrified. He thought the end had come. He began to shuffle across the room. In a panic he grabbed the sofa, and as he reached for the table, the sun came out again. The room got bright.

By accident, as he leaned there, he saw his face in the mirror by the front door. It scared him. He looked as wild as a man marooned twenty years on a desert island.

Lennie swallowed. He took a deep breath. Then slowly, his shoulders hunched forward, his chest heaving with unspent sobs, he started for the door.

**12** Lennie struggled out onto the front porch. Every step killed him. He could not even touch his wounded leg to the floor now.

He moved so slowly and carefully it almost seemed that he was not moving at all. Inch by inch he made it across the warped floor boards and caught the porch railing. He hung there for a moment, bent forward, staring down into the ferns below.

He raised his head then and looked across the lake. The sun had gotten lower in the sky. Could it already be setting? How much time *had* passed, Lennie wondered. The lake was shining with the red sun and the reflection of

65

the beech trees. Probably not more than a half hour since he had first felt that piercing sting on his ankle.

The redness of the lake seemed like a bad omen to him, a prediction of terrible things to come. It was like a prophecy. When the waters of the earth turn red . . .

Someone he knew had believed in omens. Who was it? His Grandmother Madison probably. When the caterpillars were thick, a bad winter was coming. When an owl cried in the night, somebody was going to die. What would she say about this? When the waters of the earth turn red . . .

Or maybe it was his Grandfather Madison. No, his Grandfather Madison had been an old man who ran motels and in his spare time worked at making concrete figures to adorn them.

The thing his Grandfather Madison believed in was not complaining. One time when Lennie had broken his arm and was crying because the cast itched, his Grandfather Madison had told him that there was an old legend that said birds were created without wings. When their wings were put on their bodies as a punishment, the birds complained, but as soon as they stopped complaining, the wings grew to their bodies and lifted them into the air.

Lennie had been so puzzled about what this had to do with the cast on his arm that he had stopped crying at once. He still didn't understand it.

Lennie's leg jerked again. The pain was so sharp and sudden that Lennie threw back his head like an animal. He felt like howling, but instead he yelled, "Does anybody hear me?"

He waited, listened to the silence, and then tried again. *"Will somebody please help me?"* He paused. *"I'm over here at the stone house!"*

Nobody answered, and the silence frightened Lennie. It was a total silence. He couldn't even hear any birds or crickets. The leaves had stopped turning in the trees.

It was as if he really were the last person on earth. Even Friend couldn't help him. Remember, Friend had surrendered to the police. In a flash a picture came to Lennie of Friend sitting in a cell at the station, his batteries gradually getting weaker. ("Don't forget, kids, to keep spare batteries handy so you'll never be without a Friend.") By the time the police got around to questioning him, his voice would be too faint to hear.

"Speak up, son, tell us your name in a good loud voice."

Hmmmmmm

"I said for you to speak *up!* If you don't, we're going to have to take some action."

Hmm

The silence continued. Even the water no longer lapped at the shore.

Lennie glanced down at his leg. It was swelling now, the skin tight and shiny, and as hot as if it were on fire. His leg twitched again, frog-like, and the pain almost made him faint.

His strength was leaving him rapidly. He was so weak now that he had to sit down or he would collapse. Moving his leg as little as possible, Lennie eased himself down on the top step. With a sigh, he reclined against the porch railing.

After a moment, even weaker, he let himself lie on the porch. He sagged. All his strength was gone. His leg felt like a sausage in a frying pan.

He looked up at the porch ceiling. Rain had seeped through the tar and shingles of the roof and stained the boards. Lennie saw it all in a kind of blur because he had started crying again.

All of a sudden Lennie found himself remembering a poem. Lennie knew only one poem. He had had to learn it for a school assignment.

"If everyone else can memorize a poem, you can too, Lennie," his teacher had said.

"But why can't I substitute a TV jingle? They're poems. They rhyme."

"No, Lennie."

"But listen to this. Why isn't this a poem?

"Hold the pickle, hold the lettuce,
Special orders don't upset us,
All we ask is that you let us
Serve you—"

"No, Lennie, that's not poetry."

"Well, here's another one. What's wrong with this?

"Hotdogs, Armour hotdogs.
What kind of kids like Armour hotdogs?
Fat kids, skinny kids, kids who—"

"Lennie, for the last time, you are to learn a *poem*. Advertising jingles are not poetry."

Lennie could no longer remember the teacher's name —he had had twenty-three different teachers in all that year—but he could still remember his poem and how bright the sun had been, slanting into the room, as he said it. It was as if the audience were lit up for the occasion instead of the stage.

"The July sun is gone,
   The August moon.
   September's stars are dim,
   October's bright noon."

"I am curious," the teacher had said when he had finished. "Why did you select that particular poem, Lennie?"

He had selected it because all the months of the year were in it, and that would make it easier to memorize. He already knew the months. "It just appealed to me," he had said.

"Why, Lennie?"

"I don't know."

"What do you think the poet had in mind when he wrote the poem?" The teacher, interested in Lennie for the first time, crossed in front of her desk.

"Let me think." Lennie put his hand to his chin at this point to give the impression of deep thought. Lennie had always had a hard time arranging his face in the right expression. Looking interested or studious was especially hard for him. He sometimes thought he needed acting lessons on being a person.

"Do you think he was just talking about *one* year passing?" the teacher went on. "Or do you think, Lennie, that the poet was seeing his whole life as a year, that he was seeing his whole life slipping past?"

"I'm not sure." Lennie's hand was still on his chin as if ready to stroke a long gray beard.

"Class?"

"*His whole life slipping past,*" the class chorused together. They had had this teacher so long that they could tell, just from the way she asked a question, what they were supposed to answer.

"I was just getting ready to say that," Lennie mumbled into his hand.

And now, two years too late, Lennie knew what they were talking about. The poet *had* meant his whole life. Lennie knew because he saw his whole life slipping away too. In exactly the same way. July's sun. August's moon. September's stars. October's noon.

He closed his eyes and the tears came again, hot and fast. He couldn't remember the rest of the poem. What was it he would miss about November and December? He squeezed his eyes shut tighter in determination. He stuck out his jaw.

Then his body went slack. He sighed. He realized that he would miss everything about the world. He would miss all the reruns of *Bonanza* and *Star Trek*. He would miss shows that hadn't even come on the air, midwinter replacements he didn't even know about. He would miss shows that hadn't even been thought up yet. He would miss his mother.

Lennie sighed again. And his mother would miss him. That was the worst thought. To get his mind off it, he tried to think of something he had seen on TV. All the programs were a blur. He couldn't even remember what dangers Mannix had faced last week, or Columbo. And Kojak had been in real trouble. What was it?

He groaned, feeling again the pain of separation from his mother.

All Lennie's life his own feelings had been as hard to get to as the meat in a walnut. His feelings were there—Lennie was sure of that—somewhere inside the hull, probably just as perfectly formed as the rest of the things nature put in a shell.

Lennie remembered that one March morning he and his mom had been burning trash behind the motel. His mom had said, "Why, Lennie, look at this."

Lennie had come over to where his mom was standing by some bushes. "What is it?"

"It's an old cocoon. We'll take it in and cut it open, and you can see where a butterfly grew."

His mom had broken off the twig and, forgetting the trash fire, had gone into the motel. She had taken her onion knife and sawed through the cocoon. "There," she had said.

For a moment Lennie and his mom had stared at the cut-open cocoon in silence. Then his mom had said in a sad voice, "Oh, dear. It wasn't empty. I cut through a butterfly."

Lennie had stared silently at the two halves, the pale wet center.

"It was the first cocoon I ever saw. I'm sorry, Lennie."

He could see that it really bothered her, and he'd said, "That's all right."

"I just didn't know."

Lennie felt that his own feelings had suddenly been laid bare in the same way. Now that it was too late, he found that— He broke off. He had just remembered the last part of the poem.

> And November's morn
> White with frost
> And December's snows
> Are melted and lost.

Anyway, it was something like that.

**13** Trying to remember the lines of the poem had helped Lennie forget his pain for a moment. It seemed to him then that if you knew enough poems to say to yourself, you could get through anything. He tried to think of something else to divert him. He went back to TV. TV jingles maybe.

> I'd like to teach the world to sing
>   In perfect harmony
>   I'd like to hold it in my hands
>   And keep it company.
> It's the reeeeeal thing, Coke is—

Lennie moaned. They weren't as good as poetry.

Quaker State your caaaaaaaar,
To keep it running young,

Maybe they were too easy to remember.

Oh, Log Cabin makes good syrups,
'Bout the best as anyone can.
Whether regular or buttered—

Abruptly his leg jerked and he couldn't think of anything but the pain. He raised up and looked at his leg.
Grimacing with the pain, he looked down the slope to
the willow trees. He could see the edge of his boat through
the trees. He took a deep breath.

Double your pleasure, double your fun,
With double—

It wouldn't work. He looked again at his boat. He
thought, maybe if I can reach the boat I can float across
the lake. Then maybe I can crawl real slowly through
the field. Then maybe I can . . . He saw it as if it were
happening on television. It seemed possible.

He leaned up on one elbow. He hesitated, struggling
with himself. Lassie would make it, he told himself. A
rattlesnake bite wouldn't stop Lassie. A shark bite wouldn't
stop Flipper. Gentle Ben would drag a bear trap a hundred miles to save himself.

Lennie took a deep breath and tried to push himself into a sitting position. He fell back on his elbow. He tried again. He couldn't make it.

He was very weak now, but he wanted desperately to be in his boat floating toward home. He could almost feel himself moving over the gentle waves. He tried to push himself up again. He failed. He lay back on the porch.

The silence around him was awful now. It wasn't only the silence that bothered Lennie. It was the terrible feeling that everything had stopped moving. The sun wasn't dropping in the sky. It was still hanging in the sky in exactly the same place. The wind wasn't blowing. The clouds weren't moving. The trees were as still as plastic arrangements.

He closed his eyes. He had lost track of time. He didn't know how long he had been lying here. It seemed like days. Years. Centuries.

He felt as if he had been lying here long enough to have been frozen in a glacier or petrified by burning lava. He had been lying here long enough to be preserved and sent to some museum as the main display.

He would be more popular in the museum than the mummy or the fossilized whale. "Hey, did you guys see the preserved kid?"

"No, where's any preserved kid?"

"Around yonder. He's ten million years old—the card says so, and he's got a snake bite on his ankle. You can even see the holes.

"Where? Show me."

"Come on if you don't believe me."

He would be so popular that they would make a whole educational TV program about him, Lennie thought. They would reconstruct his life, his last day. The show would be called "This Is the Way We Think It Was," and as the young actor lay stretched out, imitating Lennie's pain, imitating Lennie's dying, the announcer's voice would say, "Yes, this is the way we think it was, ten million years ago today."

Lennie raised his head. The only bit of movement left in the world was his pounding heart. And now even that seemed to be slowly winding down.

Lennie stretched out flat on the porch. His mind drifted back in time. He thought of a friend he had had in Nashville. Nashville was the only place he and his mom had stayed long enough for Lennie to get a good friend. The other places they had lived, by the time people got used to Lennie and stopped picking on him, right then he and his mom had moved.

This friend in Nashville was Carl Lee Norton, and he and Lennie used to walk home from school together through an old cow field. They both lived in side-by-side trailers in Pineview Trailer Court. And sometimes when they got tired, they would lie down in the field and just look up at the sky.

One day as they were lying there in silence, an airplane flew overhead, a small plane, white and red, single engine. Lennie, watching the plane, began to will it to fall from the sky. "Fall! Fall! Fall!" he was saying to himself, not really wanting the plane to fall, just testing his ability to make things happen.

At that very moment, as Lennie lay there with his brain powers trained on the airplane, Carl Lee sat up and said, "Hey, I bet that's my uncle."

"Where?"

"Up there in that airplane. You know, Uncle David. It looks like his Cessna."

"Oh."

Lennie lay back and closed his eyes. He felt weak. He realized he had been willing one of his most admired people, Carl Lee's Uncle David, the man who had let Lennie sit in the cockpit of his glider and promised to take him up in an airplane—*this* was the man he had been willing to fall from the sky.

"I got to go home," he said after a moment. He got up slowly. The plane was out of sight, hopefully still flying.

"Me too," Carl Lee said.

And the two of them walked toward their trailers with the matching plastic sofas and the plastic sliding doors and the carpets of miracle fibers. As he entered his trailer, Carl Lee called, "I'll ask Uncle David if we can go up in his Cessna this Sunday."

Lennie nodded, but he wasn't so eager to go up any more. Going up in the airplane was ruined now. Because maybe, just maybe, there would be some other person, in some other field, looking up at the sky, saying, "Fall! Fall! Fall!" to Lennie's plane. Sure, he, Lennie, didn't have any power, but maybe somebody else did.

But now, lying on the porch, dying, he sent out a mental signal to the world. Come! Come! Come! Silently he willed the invisible people with all his might. Anyone within range of my mind, come! Help me! Help!

His leg jerked again, and he cried out. He put his fists up to his eyes.

"You have to keep hold of yourself," his mother had told him once. It was just after her boyfriend Sam had died. Lennie had been sad too. Sam was his favorite of his mother's boyfriends. Sam had owned a diner and was so big and strong he flattened hamburgers like he was swatting flies. He was always saying, "Hit me, kid, go ahead and hit me hard as you can."

Lennie would hit and hit until his arms got tired, but it was like trying to hurt a mattress. Lennie liked it when he couldn't hurt Sam. It was nice to know that there was one person in the world who could not be hurt no matter what you did.

And then Sam had died. He died right at the diner while he was shoveling snow off the parking lot. His heart, it turned out, was not as strong as his body.

Lennie had sat in the last booth with his mom while she warmed her hands around a cup of coffee.

"You always have to keep hold of yourself," she said.

Lennie had a young-looking mother. People were always mistaking her for his sister. Now for the first time she looked old enough to really be his mother.

She wrapped her arms around herself. "Never let go, Lennie."

"I try not to."

"No matter what happens."

"Will we have to leave the diner?"

She nodded.

"But where will we go?"

"I don't know, but if we just keep hold of ourselves we'll be all right."

"I'll try to."

Now, as if to keep his word, Lennie hugged himself. One hand was on each shoulder, but his fingers were like icy claws. There was no comfort. He wished for dream arms that would grow long on command and wrap him like soft fleshy hoses.

Holding himself tighter, he sent out the message again. Somebody, anybody, come.

14 A sound broke through the stillness of the front porch. Lennie couldn't place the noise at first, but he waited. He held his breath and listened.

Maybe the sound hadn't been real, he thought. It was puzzling. It was like the time his mother had taken him to the wax museum in New Orleans. The wax museum had been a substitute treat because they hadn't been able to find Midget City. "All right," his mother had said finally, "we'll just go to the wax museum. You want to see wax people, don't you?"

They had gone in, and Lennie had really been surprised at how real the people looked. Lennie could see the pores in their hands. Their eyes looked right at him.

Still and all, there had been something wrong, something so wrong that Lennie couldn't really be scared, no matter how hard he tried, not even in the Chamber of Horrors. It just wasn't real somehow.

That was the same feeling Lennie had now as he lay on the porch, thinking back on the sound he had heard. He listened. Now he couldn't hear anything at all.

It seemed to him that maybe the sound had been a car door slamming, but he wasn't sure. Maybe it was just because that was what he wanted it to be. He tried to pull himself up on his elbow.

"Help me," he called out. "Is anybody there?" He waited. "I'm here on the porch. I'm dying."

His hopes went up and down like a pop fly. He sank back to the porch. He didn't have the strength to hold his head up any more. He called again, but his voice seemed to be no more than a sigh.

"Somebody help me," he begged. For a moment his hopes were all mixed up with the wax figures in New Orleans, and he imagined that Napoleon and Huey Long and Flip Wilson were drawing around him.

Abruptly he turned his head from side to side as if to clear it of a bad dream. He wet his lips. He murmured, "No," to the wax figures. "No!"

Then he grew still. He had heard another sound. It was real. Someone had spoken to him.

"Son?"

Lennie's eyes snapped open. He tried to rise again. The big sagging cop was standing at the bottom of the steps, tall as a tree.

Lennie blinked. He saw the policeman clearly now. Lennie drew in a breath of air. His heart rested a moment. He said, "Help me."

"Sure, son, what happened to your leg?"

"Snake bite."

"What kind of snake, son—do you know?"

"Rattler." Saying the word made him shiver. His leg jerked again and he cried out.

The big cop straightened. "Hey, Bert," he called, "get the hospital on the double."

"My leg's on fire," Lennie moaned.

"Tell them a kid's been bit by a rattlesnake," he yelled. "We're bringing him in. Then get over here and help me."

"My mom—" Lennie began.

"Yeah, son, who is your mom?"

"She runs the Fairy Land Motel."

"We'll get your mom—now you just lie quiet. When did it happen, son—can you tell me?"

"It was right after you drove off the second time."

"We knew you were there. We saw your wet footprints on the front porch."

Lennie nodded. The boat leaked, his sneakers were wet, he had left his footprints.

His leg twitched again, and the hot pain shot through his whole body. He began to cry.

"Don't cry, son. We're going to get you to the hospital. Won't take us five minutes."

"I can't help crying."

"I know. A buddy of mine got snake-bit—we were on

a picnic down at Wandover Falls, and my buddy was reaching in the grass for a baseball, and the snake caught him on his little finger, right there, by the nail. My buddy cried too, and he was a grown man, forty years old."

Lennie groaned.

"Give me a hand here, Bert," the big cop said. "I'll steady his leg." They got Lennie into lifting position. "Here we go."

Lennie cried out as they picked him up—his leg couldn't stand the slightest touch now—and then he felt himself being rushed to the car.

"Can you get the door?" the big cop asked.

"Yeah."

As they struggled with the door, Lennie stared up through the golden leaves of the trees. He saw a moon in the late afternoon sky. It was white. A children's moon they called it when it came out like that in the daytime. Lennie's grandfather had told him so. There was a story connected with it, but Lennie didn't feel like remembering it. He moaned as they slid him into the back seat.

"Now, you just stretch out there and try to relax. You all right?"

"I don't know," Lennie groaned.

"I'll stay back here with you," the big cop said. "Bert, you drive."

He crawled in and sat on the edge of the seat. He said, "I wish we'd found you the first time we came by. Then this wouldn't have happened."

"I do too," Lennie said.

"Where were you?"

"Under the house." Lennie turned his head away. "I didn't know snakes stayed under houses."

"I reckon they do." The car started. "Here we go," the big cop said.

**15** Lennie glanced out the car window, and he got one last look at the stone house. It was just a gray-and-brown blur now. It had nothing to do with him. It wasn't *his* house, any more than a theater he had watched a movie in was his theater, or a diner he had had a meal in was his diner.

It was strange the way objects could be valuable one moment and worthless the next. It was the way colored Easter eggs seem like real gold when you're on a hunt, running through the grass with an empty basket swinging at your side. And then the next day one of those same colored eggs can be just a cracked smelly object.

"How're you doing, son?" the big cop asked.

Lennie closed his eyes as if to shut out the question. "I don't know."

"You just hang in there."

"That's what I'm trying to do." Lennie wet his dry lips. Without opening his eyes, he said, "What happened to your friend that got bit by the rattlesnake? Did he die?"

"Naw, he didn't die. That was old Hank Thompson, Bert—you remember him. Big fellow. Used to coach Little League. He missed two weeks of work, as I recall it, and he never has stuck his hand down in deep grass again."

"I'll never crawl under another house," Lennie said, moaning a little as they went over a bump.

"They used to tease him about it. 'Get the ball, Hank,' they'd call. 'It's right over there in the *grass.*'" He smiled. "Hank would back up a mile to keep from touching a clump of grass. He'd always say, 'One rattlesnake bite'll do me for the rest of my life.'"

"That's true," Lennie moaned.

As they got to the highway, the siren started up. It sounded different, Lennie thought, when it was *you* inside the car, when it was *you* that the trucks and cars were going to pull over to the side of the road for. He tried to raise his head and see if it was happening. He was too weak.

"You all right, son?"

Lennie opened his eyes. He looked at the big cop. He nodded.

88

"Well, just hold on."

Lennie kept looking at the big cop's face. Suddenly he thought of the time his mom had taken him down the street in Nashville to see a man who was buried alive. The man was buried in a special box, and there was a green awning over it. For a dime you could look down a tube and speak to the man who was buried below.

Lennie would never forget looking down the tube. He had had a million questions he wanted to ask, but as soon as he saw the man's face below him, he couldn't say a word.

"Ask him how long he's going to stay down there," his mother had prompted.

"How long are you going to stay down there?"

"As long as the people of Nashville want me to," the man had answered.

"Ask him how he eats."

"How do you eat?"

But the woman taking up the dimes had said, "Move on now, these girls want to see too." And Lennie had to move on and make room for three girls who were already arguing over who would have to look first.

Lennie had moved on, but it had left him with a funny sensation, looking at a stranger through a tube like that. Because for a moment the stranger's face had blotted out the whole world. It had just been the stranger and Lennie.

Lennie had thought everybody should have to look at everybody else at least once through a tube. You could see them so much more clearly.

Now Lennie could see the big cop in the same clear, one-to-one way. Lennie said, "Tell me about your friend some more, your friend that got bit."

"Well, let's see. He lost his fingernail—I remember that."

"What did they do to him at the hospital?"

"Well, they gave him some shots, as I recall it, and something to take away the pain. He was real happy to be in the hospital—" He broke off. "Pull in here, Bert, this is the emergency entrance."

The big cop turned back to Lennie. "We'll get you inside and you'll be fine."

In Lennie's mind the big cop suddenly got mixed up with Sam. Maybe it was because they were both so big. Lennie half expected the big cop to turn around and say, "Hit me in the stomach, kid." Lennie put out his hand and held tightly to the cop's sleeve. "I want you to carry me, not him."

"All right." Bert opened the door. Awkwardly the big cop climbed out and reached back to help Lennie. "Let's go."

**16** "Antivenom test was negative," a voice was saying.

Lennie was lying with his eyes closed. He was sobbing to himself. He opened his eyes once to see if the big cop was still standing in the doorway. The big cop lifted his hand and said to Lennie, "Your mom'll be here in a minute. Bert's gone to get her."

Lennie turned away. He closed his eyes. His body shook with sobs.

"Just hold on," the cop called.

Lennie felt himself being given shots all over his body. It was just another pain. Then they were making slits in his legs, and just when he thought it was all over, he got two more shots, one in the ankle and one in the thigh, then two more in the hip. He lost count.

Somebody said, "We gave you something to ease the pain. You should be feeling some relief soon."

They rolled him out of the emergency room, down the green hall, and into the elevator.

"I'll stay with you till your mom gets here," the cop said.

Lennie nodded. He reached out and took the cop's hand. He was beginning to relax a little now.

"The doctors say you're going to be just fine."

"I don't know," Lennie murmured.

Two people lifted him onto a bed. Lennie reached out for the cop's hand again. He ran his free hand over the sheet like a small child comforting himself with a favorite blanket. He felt sleepy.

"Here's your mom," the big cop said.

She was standing in the doorway in blue jeans and a tie-dyed shirt. She came over to the bed and started to cry.

Lennie said, "I'm sorry."

"You don't have anything to be sorry about," she said. "You just get well."

"I shouldn't have tried to hide." His lips were dry. It was getting hard to talk.

"Don't say anything. You just rest and concentrate on getting well. You are very important to me."

His mom kept patting his arm. His mom used to play the piano long ago, but she had been taught by an aunt who could only play hymn chords, and now she was patting him with all her fingers, the same chord over and over.

Lennie felt confused. He said, "Am I still in the hospital?" The room was blurring. The green walls were moving closer.

His mom said, "Now, you just keep hold of yourself." She kept patting his arm, the same chord.

Lennie thought of his arms rising and winding around his body like ropes. He ran his fingers back and forth on the sheet.

"Try to sleep."

"I got to tell you something first," Lennie began through his dry lips, but before he had a chance to go on, he had forgotten what he wanted to say.

"No, don't talk. I understand."

Lennie sighed. It was easier, if she really did understand, not to have to tell it, whatever it was. He couldn't remember.

"What time is it?" he asked.

"Four thirty."

"When was I bit?"

"Well, they said it must have been about an hour and a half ago. You were lucky to get help that fast."

"I know."

"Now you just lie back and rest. Get well. That's all that matters. Want me to close the blinds?"

Lennie opened his eyes and saw the sun. It looked like it was setting. It didn't seem possible. He couldn't remember what day it was. Maybe, he thought, this was the longest day on record. They would put it in a book. The

longest day ever recorded was on an afternoon in early October, the day a boy was bit by a rattlesnake under a stone house at a lake.

His mother got up and closed the blinds. "There, is that better?"

"I can still smell the lake."

"No, hon, the whole hospital's air-conditioned," she said. "The window's shut tight."

"I can smell it, Mom, I tell you. I can smell it. Don't you believe me?"

"Yes, yes," his mother said, playing three quick chords on his arm. "Don't get upset, Lennie. Just lie there and try to sleep. I think I can smell the lake too."

Lennie remembered suddenly what he had wanted to tell her. "I failed my Science test," he said. "It's under my socks."

"That's all right."

"You will have to sign it."

"I will."

"It's the Science test you thought I was studying for so hard."

"That's all right."

"It's the Science test you said you were proud of me for passing."

"It's all right."

"It doesn't matter to you?"

"No."

Comforted, Lennie sighed. His mother kept patting his arm, and in a few minutes he slept.

**17** "He'll be all right, ma'am. They've made a lot of progress in snake-bite treatment." It was the big cop talking to Lennie's mother. Lennie heard him, but he didn't open his eyes for a moment. The pain was back now, as bad as before.

"I hope," his mom said.

"Folks who talk about the world going to the dogs forget all the progress we've made."

"I know," his mom said.

"Why, I read the other day that there's McDonald hamburger places in Japan now and shopping centers in India."

"We all have a lot to be thankful for."

"And your boy's going to be just fine. Living in modern times has its advantages, and one of them is that your boy's going to be all right."

"Mom," Lennie said through dry lips.

"I'm right here, Lennie." He could feel her leaning over him. He could smell her clean lemony smell.

"What time is it?"

"It's—" She paused and looked at her watch. "It's eleven forty."

"At night?"

"Yes."

"Oh."

Lennie moaned. He hadn't known pain could be this bad. The worst pain he had suffered before today was the digging out of a splinter at Sam's Diner and the setting of a broken arm in Nashville. This was a total, all-out pain.

"I don't think I'm going to get through the night," he said more to himself than to his mom.

"Yes, you will, Lennie. It'll get better. Just hold on to yourself."

"Can't they give me something for the pain?"

"They already have, hon."

"Are you sure?"

"They've given you all they can. It'll ease up soon."

"I know it won't." He began to cry. "Pain like this doesn't ease."

"It *will*."

He lay with his eyes closed for a moment, tears rolling down his cheeks. Then he said, "What time is it?"

98

"It's"—she paused—"eleven forty-one."

"Oh." He lay without moving. He was trying to last just five more minutes. He could no longer think of getting through the whole night. Five more minutes was the best he could do. "What time is it *now?*"

"It's eleven forty-two."

"Oh." Four more minutes to go.

The big cop—Lennie had forgotten he was in the room —said, "I'll go speak to the nurse. Maybe she can do something."

"I'd appreciate it." After the cop left the room, his mother said, "You want to talk, Lennie? Maybe it would help you get your mind off the pain."

"I'll try."

"Want me to tell you about the time I was in the hospital? I was just about your age."

"All right."

"It was an accident."

"Car?"

"No, I was climbing a tree behind the motel—"

"Our motel?"

"No, this was a different one. It was in Kentucky, and it was called the Kosy K. We lived in one of the cabins. Kosy K Kabins was the full name. Anyway, I was out back climbing an old oak tree and I fell. I landed in the crook of the tree on my knee, and I broke that, and then I fell on the ground and broke my arm."

"Oh."

"And they took me to the hospital in the back of an old pickup truck. I can still remember how scared I was because I had never even spent a night away from home."

"Oh," Lennie said. He paused, wet his lips. "What time is it now?"

"It's"—pause—"eleven forty-four."

One more minute to go, Lennie thought.

"You want to hear the rest about my arm?"

"Yeah, go on."

"Well, the knee wasn't too bad, but the arm got infected. See, the bone had poked through the skin, and they thought I was going to die, Lennie. I was in the hospital for two and a half weeks. It almost caused me to fail fifth grade." She broke off as the cop came back in the room.

"The nurse'll be in in a minute," he said.

"Did you hear that, Lennie? Hold onto yourself because the nurse is coming."

"What time is it now?" Lennie asked.

"It's eleven forty-six."

He had made it. Five minutes. And he was already one minute into the next five.

His mom said, "Officer Olson was just telling me while you were asleep, Lennie, that a friend of his got bit by a rattlesnake on his little finger."

"Oh."

"I told him about it, ma'am."

"And, Lennie, he says he'll get the man to come see you tomorow if it'll make you feel better."

Lennie nodded. He waited as long as he could stand it and then he said, "What time is it now?"

**18** That was how Lennie got through that first night—five minutes and then five minutes more. It seemed to Lennie that the night, separated into those five-minute periods, was longer than the whole rest of his life. He would never have believed that five minutes could be longer than a year, but now he knew it was true.

In the morning when the doctor came in to look at Lennie's leg and to change the dressing, Lennie was past caring. He didn't even want to get well any more.

"How are you feeling?" the doctor asked.

Lennie just shook his head.

"Well, let's see that leg."

Lennie closed his eyes and moaned. His leg hurt so bad he could even feel the doctor's breath on his knee. It was like a blowtorch.

"Don't get near my leg," Lennie murmured as he fainted.

He didn't remember anything else about the rest of the morning except that it was one terrible pain after another.

In the afternoon the big cop came in. He leaned on the foot of the bed. "Remember me telling you about my friend that got snake bit?" he said. "Well, here he is!" The cop sounded as cheerful as if he'd done a feat of magic.

Lennie tried. He opened his eyes. He blinked to clear his vision. He made an effort to see the man beside his bed.

"There's my finger that got bit," the man said, leaning over Lennie's bed. "See? You can still see the scars, and here are the slits they had to make in my hand to relieve the swelling. Here, here, here, here, and here. And my fingernail's gone." He wagged his little finger. "See? No fingernail!"

Lennie tried to focus his eyes on the finger and the slits, but he didn't care any more. Nothing mattered. He closed his eyes.

"He would be real glad to see you if he wasn't feeling so bad," his mother said.

"Well, we'll come back, son, don't worry about it. To-morrow or the next day I'll bring him back," the cop said.

"He'll feel more like looking at the finger then," his mom said. She turned to Lennie. "And, Lennie, did you see what Officer Olson brought you? It's a clock! Now you won't have to ask for the time so much. It's an electric clock, and you can read it as easy as a sign."

There was a silence while everyone waited for Lennie's reaction.

Then his mother said, "I'm sure he'd thank you if he was feeling better."

"Why, that's all right. He don't have to thank me," the cop said.

"Well, I'm sure he would if he could."

Lennie glanced at the clock. It *was* nice. Any other time it would have pleased him. The numbers rolled into view on a special dial. The numbers said 3:45. Then, slowly, 3:46 rolled into view.

"Thank you for coming," his mom said.

"Ma'am, I wouldn't have missed it," the man said. He was still holding out his little finger like he was drinking tea. "I know what it's like to be snake-bit, believe you me."

Lennie didn't remember anything else about that afternoon except that after supper the doctor came in and changed the dressing and had to make some more slits in Lennie's leg.

"I'm going to give you something for the pain, Lennie, but it's going to hurt. You're going to have to be a brave boy," the doctor said.

"He will be," his mother said.

Lennie was already crying. Just the mention of any more pain than he was suffering now was more than he could bear.

"Now, Lennie, get hold of yourself, please, honey," his

mother said. Then she turned to the doctor. "He's usually real brave about everything. The time he had his arm set he never even moaned."

But bravery didn't seem important to Lennie now. Nothing was. He yelled and cried and hollered. He hit at the doctor until the nurse had to hold his hands. He cursed. He screamed. He sobbed as if he would never stop.

"Now, it's all over," the doctor said. "That wasn't so bad, was it?"

His mother was coming back into the room. "See, hon, it's all over. Things will be better now. I'm just real sure things'll be better."

"The nurse will give you something to help you sleep now," the doctor said. "In the morning you should be feeling some better."

The only thing Lennie remembered about the next morning was that he saw his leg for the first time. It scared him so much that for a moment even the pain stopped.

His leg no longer even resembled a leg. It was a huge swollen object, shiny as glass. "Oh, no," he moaned. From his thigh to his toes, his leg was twice as big as normal, and it was every color in the rainbow.

Lennie fell weakly back on his pillow. "I told you not to look," the nurse said. "Now you lie back and relax."

"Where's my mom?" Lennie asked weakly.

"She stepped out in the hall for a minute."

"I want my mom." The sight of his leg had made him weak and sick and scared. He tried to rise. "Mom!"

"She'll be back in just a minute, soon as the doctor gets through. Your mom just felt a little dizzy and needed some air."

"Oh." The nurse eased him back against his pillow. Lennie knew that the sight of his leg had been too much for his mother, too. He remembered she went out in the hall every time it was uncovered.

"It's beginning to look some better," the doctor said.

"Not to me," Lennie moaned. "I never want to see my leg again."

But to everyone else the leg was a fascinating sight. That was what Lennie remembered most about the next two days—showing his leg. Nurses from other floors, doctors, patients who were allowed to walk around, visitors, all came in to have a look at Lennie's leg.

"Haven't they ever seen a leg before?" he kept asking the nurse.

"Not like that one," she said. "You couldn't get any more color on that leg with a paintbrush."

"Will it ever go away?"

"Oh, sure."

"When?"

"Oh, by next week probably."

"Next week?" Lennie moaned. It seemed a lifetime. Turning his head to the window, he began to weep.

**19** It was Friday before Lennie felt like he really wanted to live. That happened about four o'clock in the afternoon. Lennie's mom had rented a TV set for him to watch, and she had just rolled up the head of his bed so he could see. A rerun of *Bonanza* was on.

And as Lennie lay there watching Hoss win a Chinese girl in a poker game, he suddenly felt hungry. The hunger surprised him for a moment. Up until now he hadn't wanted a thing to eat. They had had to feed him through a tube in his arm.

He said, "Mom, I'm hungry."

106

His mom was watching Hoss, smiling because Hoss had thought he was winning a *horse* named Ming Lee. Now he was afraid to take the *girl* Ming Lee back to the Ponderosa and show her to Pa. His mom turned her head to Lennie and got up at the same time. "I'll get you something to eat," she said quickly.

At the door she turned, still smiling, and said, "The nurse will be so pleased. She's been trying to get Jell-O and broth down you for days."

"I know, Mom, but I don't want that stuff."

"What do you feel like eating then? I'll go out for something if the doctor says you can have it."

"I want a hamburger."

"Oh, Lennie, I don't think—"

"And a chocolate shake."

"Well, I'll try, but I really don't—"

"And if they won't let me have that, then I'll take a pizza."

"I'll try, Lennie."

He lay back down. He already knew he wasn't going to get the hamburger or the pizza. His mom was going to come back with Jell-O and broth, but it didn't much matter. He felt hungry enough to eat anything.

A commercial came on the screen. A little girl was swinging, and a solemn voice announced that the little girl had skinned her knee yesterday and was about to fall on the same knee today.

Lennie looked at the girl's knee. There was a mark the size of a dime. He glanced down at his own huge, dis-

107

colored leg. He thought that the people who made television commercials didn't know anything about real life, not the way he, Lennie, did.

It seemed to him suddenly that every TV person he had ever seen wasn't real, not the girl in danger of skinning her knee again, not the women who had just given up their soap for an experiment in white clothes, not the man who had eaten enchiladas and gotten an acid stomach.

Lennie went on, even including his favorites. Not Hoss, who had just won a Chinese girl in a poker game. Not Lassie, who had rescued a colt from a burning barn. Not Gentle Ben, who didn't really kill the chickens. Not the Brady Bunch, who had to go on a talent show and sing a rock song to get money for their parents' anniversary gift.

That wasn't life. It was close enough to fool you, Lennie thought, if you weren't careful, and yet those TV characters were as different as a wax figure is from a real person. Lennie imagined you had to come up against life hard to know what it was all about.

He looked at the TV. He smiled slightly. On the screen Hoss was saying, "But, dagburnit, Pa, how was *I* to know Ming Lee was a girl?"

Lennie watched Pa for a moment. Pa Cartwright was the kind of father that would make you think—if you had a father—that your father wasn't good enough. Or Lassie pulling a newborn colt from the burning barn made you think your dog wasn't good enough. Or Mother Nature–

type forests ruined real forests for you, made them seem dirty and empty. Or the Waltons or the Brady Bunch made you think there was something wrong with your family, when really, Lennie thought, his own family—just him and his mom—was a hundred times realer than the Bradys or the Waltons or the Cleavers or any other TV family you could name.

Lennie shifted on his hospital bed. After his mother brought his supper, he thought, he would turn off the TV for a while and work on his report. It was the only thing that really interested him. His teacher, Miss Markham, had come to see him in the hospital and had suggested that he do a report on rattlesnakes and rattlesnake bites. She would, she had said, give him extra credit for it. It would make up for his last Science test.

He had wanted to start the report right away, but he hadn't felt like it. Now, suddenly, he did.

Lennie looked at his clock. He decided he would work on his report during *Let's Make a Deal*. For a second he had a feeling of betrayal. All those people in their farmer suits and banana costumes would be in place, waiting. Monty Hall would be coming down the aisle. A great cheer would go up. Signs would wave. People would beg Monty to choose them. And Lennie would dial them all down to a small dot and start working on his report.

And after that he would betray the celebrities on *Hollywood Squares* who were waiting with their funny answers.

And after that . . .

Lennie's mother came in the door with a tray. She was smiling. "The nurse says no hamburgers or pizza today."

"What is it?"

"It's Jell-O and broth, but she says you can have something else tomorrow if you're feeling better."

"A hamburger?"

"We'll see." She sat by his bed, spooned up some broth and fed it to him. She said, "What happened on *Bonanza* while I was gone?"

"I don't know," Lennie said. "I was thinking."

"Oh?" She fed him some more broth. She dabbed at his face with a napkin. "What about?"

"My report." The broth felt good and warm inside him. "I'm going to work on it after supper."

"Now, the doctor says you shouldn't do anything you don't feel like doing."

He nodded, took another spoonful of broth. "I feel like it," he said.

**20** Lennie stood in front of the Fairy Land Motel. He was beside the wishing well. One hand was on Humpty Dumpty's head. He leaned forward and looked down at the painted water below. There were still seven pennies and one nickel, but the Mound wrapper was gone.

Lennie eased himself down on the edge of the well. His grandfather had made this well, Lennie thought, and painted all the fairyland figures. Lennie could remember how proud his grandfather had been. He glanced around. Now there were only three figures in good enough condition to be in front of the motel—one elf, Humpty Dumpty, and Hansel. But once the whole lawn had been covered. People had had their pictures taken there as if it were Disneyland.

"Mom, get a shot of me with the dwarfs."

"Dad, take me with the Wicked Witch."

Lennie ran his hand over the rim of the well. It was odd how different things looked to him now. The motel was more a home to him now than any house he could imagine. Driving up to the door after he had left the hospital had made him understand why his mom was always singing songs about going home. It had given him such a peaceful feeling to go into his room and lie down on his own bed.

Lennie straightened. He imagined that if he went back to the stone house by the lake, that would look different too. Maybe someday he would do that—go back the way other people returned to look at their old high schools or the places where they had been born.

Using his crutches, Lennie got up and walked across the driveway. He passed the cold-drink machine. Behind him the red neon sign flashed on. FAIRY LAND MOTEL— VACANCY.

Lennie's mother was watching him through the picture window of the office. She had just turned on the sign, and she came to the door. "Lennie, are you all right?"

"I'm fine, Mom."

"Well, you're supposed to take it easy."

"The doctor said I could do anything I felt like doing," he called.

"Well, *I* want you to take it easy. You're a very lucky boy. Everyone at the hospital says so."

"I know."

"Don't undo all the doctor's good work now and have a relapse."

"I won't."

A relapse was the last thing he wanted to have. By the time he got out of the hospital he had been jabbed with needles and stuck with thermometers and had his blood pressure taken enough times to last him forever.

A truck passed on the highway, building up speed for the hill ahead, and at the same time a car turned in the motel driveway. Lennie glanced around.

It was a policeman's car, and the big cop who had helped Lennie—Officer Olson—was behind the wheel. The car pulled up by Lennie.

"Well, how are things going today?" the policeman asked.

"Lots better," Lennie said. "I'm still sore from all those shots, though."

"How many did you have—did you ever find out?"

"Sixty-one. The nurse counted them for me from my chart."

"That's a lot. How's the leg?"

Lennie held it out. "I can walk around on it now. I don't even use my crutches in the house."

"Well, that's fine. You'll be ready to go on that fishing trip with me before long. I haven't forgotten my promise."

Lennie nodded.

"Your mom around?"

"In the office."

The policeman parked his car in the slot for Room 316

and got out. His jacket was open and his stomach hung over his belt. He stood for a moment, looking over the grounds. "Grass could use a cutting," he said.

"That's my job," Lennie said. "I'll probably be back at it next week the way I'm going."

He nodded. "You know, you folks got a nice place out here, real peaceful."

"Homelike," Lennie said.

The policeman went into the motel office, and Lennie hobbled across the walkway. He sat down in one of the plastic webbed chairs. He stretched out his leg. He looked at the empty chair across from him.

Suddenly he thought of Friend. "Yes, with Friend—the doll that's as big and as real as you are—you'll never be alone again."

He shifted in his chair. Not so long ago, he recalled, Friend had seemed like a pretty good idea. The way toys like G. I. Joe seem great when you see six kids playing with them on TV, laughing, having a wonderful time with about a hundred dollars' worth of extra equipment and perfectly formed little hills and cliffs and sand dunes. You don't even realize that you'll be playing on the sidewalk, probably by yourself, with no extra equipment at all. Or the way games on TV seem so much fun because they're being played by one of those TV families that do nothing but laugh together.

Why, if he had seen Friend advertised on TV, he would probably have sent off for one himself. Television could make you believe anything—it was their business.

"Only ten ninety-eight in cash or money order for

114

Friend. And remember, Friends also come in the Multi-Pack, which consists of three Friends in assorted sizes and colors so, overnight, you can become the most popular kid on your block."

Lennie would send off his money and wait. He would check the mailbox daily. He would come running in from school every day, gasping, "Anything for me?"

"Not yet, Lennie."

Then when he couldn't stand it another moment, the box would come. He would tear it open, eager to have Friend as soon as possible, eager to get on with the good times, the picnics, the long walks down country lanes, the movies.

He would lift the box top, fold back the tissue paper and there would be Friend. Lennie would be too excited to notice anything.

He would struggle with Friend, trying to get the arms and legs bent in the right position. He would get Friend on his feet. He would drag him outside. He would sit him in the other plastic webbed chair. He would begin telling Friend a joke.

A car would pass on the highway, and Lennie would imagine how he looked sitting there, laughing and joking with Friend, just like in the TV ads.

Then a little boy in the car would stick his head out the window and cry, "Hey, look, that kid's talking to a *doll!*"

Looking at the empty chair, Lennie smiled.

21 Lennie could hear the policeman and his mom talking. The policeman was saying, "After I go home and change, I'm going to come back and cut the grass. The boy shouldn't be pushing the lawn mower till he's a lot stronger."

The policeman had come to visit Lennie every single day he was in the hospital—some days he even came twice, his mom had told him.

"Did he say anything about me?" Lennie had asked when he felt good enough to worry about being caught by the police.

"Nothing bad."

"Nothing about me going in all those houses?"

"No."

"He's probably waiting till I get well."

"No, he is a very nice man, Lennie, and he's taken a real interest in you. He and his wife never had any children, so you be nice to him."

"I'll try."

"It was him got your picture in the newspaper."

Lennie *was* grateful for that. It was the first time he had ever been in the newspaper, and he had gotten twenty-nine get-well cards from people he never even heard of. And every single person in his English class had written him a note. And the mayor of the city had sent him good wishes in a letter.

A Mercury sedan turned into the motel driveway and stopped just in front of where Lennie was sitting. Lennie could hear the car radio. John Denver was singing about nature in Colorado.

The man said, "I'll check and see how much the rooms are," and he got out of the car.

There were two girls in the back seat fighting over a Young Love comic book. The older girl was saying, "Mom, I'll have you know I bought this comic with my own baby-sitting money, and I don't have to share it with anybody if I don't want to."

"Mom," the smaller girl whined, "I told her she could look at my Porky Pig, but—"

"Who wants to look at Porky Pig? Anyway, you make me sick. Everything *I* get, *you* want. Mom, she copies every single thing I do."

117

"It's flattering to be copied," the mother said in a tired voice.

"Not by *her.*"

"Now, Faye."

"I mean it. You *made* me let her wear my good pink top, and look! She's got chocolate all over it! I hate her!"

"Will you please stop it, girls? You've been arguing all the way from Tuscaloosa. Look, over there's a wishing well. Go make a wish, why don't you? I think I've got some pennies."

They took their pennies and walked to the well. The little girl looked up at her sister and said, "What are you going to wish for, Faye?"

"I'm not telling you."

"Why?"

"Because you'll wish for the exact same thing, that's why!"

They stood at the wishing well for a moment. Lennie watched them. Then silently they made their wishes and dropped their pennies into the well. The coins clanged faintly against the bottom of the well.

The man came out of the office with a key. "We're staying," he said. "Drive down to Room three-oh-two."

The policeman came out of the office right behind the man. He paused and said to Lennie, "Well, I'm taking over your job for the evening."

"What's that?"

"Grass cutting."

"Oh."

"Probably this'll be the last time it has to be cut before winter."

"Yeah."

He got in the patrol car and drove off. Lennie continued to sit in his chair.

"Hey, what's wrong with your leg?"

Lennie glanced up. It was the smaller of the sisters.

"Oh. I got bit by a rattlesnake." Lennie never said those words without a feeling of great importance coming over him. He could hardly wait to get back to school to give his report. "You want to see it?"

"Yes."

He pulled up his pants leg and showed his wounded leg. It was still colorful enough to startle.

"See all those little slit marks?" he said.

"Yes."

"They had to cut those to keep my leg from bursting open like a sausage."

"Oh." The girl's eyes got a little bigger. Her tongue came out and touched her upper lip. "Hey, Faye," she called, "he got bit by a rattlesnake. Come look."

Lennie kept his pants leg raised so that he wouldn't have to do it twice. Faye bent forward, then she turned away, one hand over her mouth. "Oh, I can't look. It must have been awful!"

"It *was* pretty bad."

"I used to think I wanted to be a nurse, but every time I see something like that, I know I couldn't. Let me see again."

"If they hadn't made those slits in his leg," the little sister said, "it would have burst open like a sausage."

"I hate snakes," Faye said, shuddering a little as she sat in the chair next to Lennie. "I think they're the awfulest things."

"You ought to read my report," Lennie said. "It's real interesting, if I did write it myself."

There was a silence, and then the little sister said, "Hey, you want to look at my Porky Pig comic book?"

"Yeah, I guess so."

"I'll go get it. It's in the car."

Faye was still looking at him. She said, "I never met anybody who got bit by a rattlesnake before."

"I've only met one other person myself," Lennie said.

"I wish I had some film in my camera. I'd take your picture."

"Oh, well," Lennie said. He leaned back in his chair. He drew the evening air into his lungs. On the highway a truck passed, building up speed for the hill ahead.

"Here it is."

Lennie held out his hand for the Porky Pig comic book. He began to flip through the pages. He glanced up and said, "You know in my report—my report about the rattlesnake—I even tell how many shots I had to have."

"How many?" the little sister asked.

Lennie looked closely at the first page of the book. Porky Pig was having to take care of the neighbor's baby. Lennie glanced up. "Sixty-one."

"*Sixty-one!*"

He nodded. He bent back over the comic book. A very small bank robber had dressed up in baby clothes to escape the cops and, without Porky Pig's knowing it, had taken the place of the baby. Porky Pig was trying to get him to take his bottle.

"When you get through with that," Faye said, "you can read my Young Love comic."

Lennie looked up at her. "*If* I have time," he said. He paused. "You see, I have to go over my report on rattlesnake bites one more time. I'm going to give it in Science class for extra credit."

"*I'*d like to hear your report," the little sister said.

"You would?" Lennie said. He had thought they would never ask. He'd begun to give up hope. "If you really want to . . ."

The girl nodded.

"Well, all right." Lennie got up quickly. He started for the motel office. He turned on his crutches. "In a lot of ways," he said, "my report is better than the stuff you see on television. It's—" He paused, searching for the right word. "It's *realer,*" he said.

Both girls nodded.

"I'll be back in a minute," Lennie said, and he went inside to get his report.